# Fairy Realm

## book 7

## The star cloak

# Fairy Realm

## the star cloak

## book 7

# EMILY RODDA

ILLUSTRATIONS BY RAOUL VITALE

HARPERCOLLINS*PUBLISHERS*

**visit us at www.abdopublishing.com**

Reinforced library bound edition published in 2008 by Spotlight, a division of the ABDO Publishing Group, Edina, Minnesota. Published by agreement with HarperCollins Children's Books.

The Star Cloak copyright © 2005 by Emily Rodda
Illustrations copyright © 2005 by Raoul Vitale

**Library of Congress Cataloging-in-Publication Data**

Rodda, Emily
    The Star Cloak / Emily Rodda ; illustrations by Raoul Vitale.
        p. cm. -- (Fairy realm ; bk. 7)
    Summary: When Giff the elf comes asking for Jessie's help, she returns to the Realm on a quest to have the fairies mend the Star Cloak in time for Wish Night.
    ISBN-13: 978-1-59961-329-1 (reinforced library bound edition)
    ISBN-10: 1-59961-329-8 (reinforced library bound edition)
    [1. Magic--Fiction. 2. Fairies--Fiction.] I. Vitale, Raoul, ill. II. Title.
PZ7.R3473Sta 2007
[Fic]--dc22

                                                                2006021989

All Spotlight books are reinforced library binding
and manufactured in the United States of America

# CONTENTS

# Fairy Realm

## BOOK 7

# The star cloak

# starry night

Jessie turned over in bed and looked at the clock on her bedside table. It was nearly midnight, but sleep was as far away as ever. She was tingling with excitement, just as she'd been ever since the first star appeared in the sky above the old house called Blue Moon.

The night sky always looked brighter in the mountains, away from the city lights. But never had Jessie seen it as it was tonight. Tonight, the moon was almost full, and the stars were *blazing*. Just looking at them made Jessie quiver.

"I don't feel sleepy at all," she'd said to her

grandmother soon after her mother had left for night duty at the hospital. "It's really weird. I feel all excited—as if something wonderful is going to happen."

Granny had raised her eyebrows in surprise. "Of course, Jessie," she'd said. "How else would you feel the night before—?" Then she'd broken off, shaking her head. "Oh, how silly of me!" she'd exclaimed. "I was thinking you knew all about it, but of course you don't! This time a year ago you and Rosemary were clearing out your house in the city, ready to move here. You missed last Wish Night."

"*Wish Night?*" Jessie had said, her eyes widening with excitement. "You mean . . . like in Grandpa's painting?"

"Oh, yes," Granny had said. "Tomorrow night, a few minutes after the first star appears, Wish Night will begin in the Realm. The stars are getting ready for it there, and even here, in the mortal world, they seem to come closer. Even here, there's magic in the air. I feel it—and so do you."

Jessie had hugged herself with excitement. No

wonder she felt as if something wonderful were about to happen. It was!

"Do you think I could go to the Realm tomorrow night?" she'd asked breathlessly. "Could I be there for Wish Night?"

Granny had laughed. "I don't see why not," she'd said, her green eyes twinkling. "In fact, I'm sure your friends are expecting you to come on the most exciting night of the Realm year. All the more reason for you to get to bed now, Jessie. It's getting late, and you might have trouble falling asleep. I always do, just before Wish Night."

*Wish Night.*

Jessie turned over in bed again, her heart fluttering as she thought of the beautiful picture that hung in the Blue Moon hallway, just near the front door. Her grandfather, Robert Belairs, had painted that picture. It was one of his most famous fairyland paintings and had been photographed for many books.

It showed a huge crowd of fairy folk and magical creatures gathered in front of a golden palace. A beautiful woman with flowing red hair, wearing a silver crown and a glittering pale blue cloak, was standing on the top of the palace steps, her arms raised. Everyone was looking up at the night sky, which was filled with falling stars that lit the darkness with flashing trails of silver light and filled the air with sparkling magic.

People visiting Blue Moon for the first time almost always stopped and looked at the painting. When at last they turned away from it they were always smiling, as if it had filled them with good feelings.

"It's called 'Wish Night,'" Granny would say when they told her how much they liked the painting. "You know that you can make a wish if you see a falling star, don't you? Well, imagine a night when the whole sky is full of them!"

Then the visitors would sigh and say what a wonderful imagination Robert Belairs must have had to think of something like that, then paint it so that it seemed so real.

Little did they know, Jessie thought, that her grandfather had painted something he'd actually seen. Little did they know that behind a hedge at the bottom of the Blue Moon garden was an invisible Door that led to the fairy world of the Realm, and that Robert Belairs had visited the Realm many, many times.

And none of them dreamed that old, white-haired Jessica Belairs, with her bright green eyes and sweet smile, was the daughter of that beautiful red-haired fairy queen in the painting. They didn't dream that more than fifty years ago a princess born to be the Realm's true queen had fallen in love with Robert Belairs and left her own world to marry him, leaving her younger sister Helena to rule in her place. That was Granny's secret—the secret only Jessie shared.

This time last year I'd only just discovered the Realm, Jessie thought. It all still seemed like a wonderful dream. Sometimes it still does!

But the Realm was no dream: the golden charm bracelet lying on Jessie's bedside table was proof of that. Every charm that hung from the bracelet had been a gift from the Realm. Every one held wonderful memories of the adventures Jessie had shared with her Realm friends: Maybelle the miniature horse, Giff the elf, and Patrice the palace housekeeper. Whenever she touched the bracelet, her mind filled with pictures of fairies, pixies, gnomes, griffins, mermaids, unicorns, Queen Helena, and the beautiful people called the Folk.

Tomorrow night I'll see Wish Night for myself, Jessie thought. I'll see the sky of the Realm filled with falling stars, just like in Grandpa's painting. And I'll be able to make a wish!

She gazed longingly at the window. There was nothing she wanted more than to pull the curtains open and look at the stars one more time.

Stop this, she told herself firmly. You've got to get some sleep. Tomorrow's a school day. If you look half-asleep in class, Ms. Stone will say you're daydreaming again and keep you in at lunchtime for another one of her "little talks."

She frowned, thinking of Ms. Stone's cool, calm voice and pale blue eyes, of Ms. Stone's smooth, fair hair drawn so tightly back from her face that her skin seemed stretched. What a contrast to their old teacher, Ms. Hewson!

Ms. Hewson had untidy, curly brown hair and

glasses that were always slipping down her freckled nose. When she laughed, or was cross, her face went bright red. Her class was sometimes noisy, but it had always been fun—or almost always. Things were very different now.

Oh, why did Ms. Hewson have to go off and have a baby! Jessie thought irritably. I *liked* Ms. Hewson. Everyone liked her. But Ms. Stone . . .

Ms. Stone wasn't a teacher anyone could actually *like*. She was young and very good-looking. Her elegant clothes always looked as if they'd just come back from the cleaners. She never raised her voice. She was well organized, calm, and logical.

But she was just *too* calm, *too* logical. It was as if she had no more feelings than a computer. She never lost her temper, but she never laughed, either. She smiled sometimes, of course, but the smile stayed at her mouth and never reached her eyes.

She also despised anything she saw as fanciful or silly or not part of the real world. This was why she hadn't chosen Jessie's story to be a finalist in the Spring Fair children's writing competition, which this year was being judged by Petra Connelly, a very well-known children's writer.

"You really must learn to use your talent more wisely, Jessica," Ms. Stone had said in her calm, cool voice. "Your little story was quite well written, but the subject — gnomes and unicorns and so on — was completely unsuitable for your age group. By now you should be writing about real people, real problems — things that matter."

My stories are about things that matter, Jessie thought fiercely. At least they matter to me! And Ms. Hewson always liked them a lot. Why shouldn't Petra Connelly like them, too?

This was no way to get to sleep. Jessie pushed the memory of Ms. Stone's voice out of her mind. She turned over again, snuggled deep under her warm quilt, and tried to think happy, peaceful thoughts.

She thought about how she loved Blue Moon, and how glad she was that she and her mother had moved from the city to live with Granny. She thought about her friend Sal, who had told her not to let old Stone-face get her down. She thought about the Realm. . . .

The old clock in the living room began to strike midnight. Dreamily, Jessie counted the chimes.

. . . nine, ten, eleven, twelve . . .

And as the last chime died away, she heard something else—something that made her sit bolt upright. Someone was tapping at her window. And there was a voice, whispering urgently.

"Jessie! Jessie!"

# problems

Her heart beating wildly, Jessie threw back the covers and jumped out of bed. She ran to the window, pulled back the curtains, and clapped a hand over her mouth to muffle a scream.

A face was pressed against the glass. Its long nose was squashed sideways. Its mouth was gaping open. Its eyes were wide with fright. There was a squeak and the face abruptly disappeared. Jessie heard a small thump.

Cautiously she opened the window and peered out. The cool night air was sweet with spring blossom. The huge trees of the Blue Moon garden whispered together beneath the starry sky. And there on the ground below the windowsill lay Giff the elf, moaning softly.

"Giff!" Jessie whispered. "Are you all right?"

"Oh dear, oh dear!" groaned Giff, slowly sitting up and rubbing his head. "Oh, Jessie, you gave me such a shock, looking out suddenly like that."

"What do you expect, if you go tapping on people's windows at midnight?" hissed Jessie. "Giff, why are you here? What's wrong?"

"Everything's wrong," Giff wailed, his pointed ears drooping so low that the tips almost touched his shoulders. "I'm in terrible trouble, Jessie. The worst trouble *ever*. You've got to help me. You've just got to!"

"Shhh!" Jessie put her finger to her lips. "Go back down to the secret garden, Giff. I'll meet you there. All right?"

Giff nodded miserably, and began feeling his legs and arms as if to check for bruises and broken bones.

Jessie closed the window and pulled on the clothes she'd left lying on her chair when she changed for bed. She fastened her charm bracelet around her wrist, then slipped from her room and tiptoed through the darkened house to the kitchen at the back. Granny had said she always had trouble sleeping just before Wish Night. If she *had* managed to fall asleep, Jessie didn't want to wake her.

Not unless I have to, anyway, she thought. If Giff's problem is really serious, I'll need to ask Granny's advice. But it probably isn't nearly as bad as he thinks. He's lost something or broken something, I suppose, but it can't be anything very important. No one lets Giff near anything really valuable.

She had expected the back door to be locked, as usual, but to her surprise it wasn't. Granny must have forgotten, she thought, letting herself out into the night. That's strange.

Then something else occurred to her. Granny's big ginger cat, Flynn, had surely heard her creeping through the house, but he hadn't come to investigate. Where was he?

"Hello there!" called a chirpy voice, making Jessie jump. "What are you doing out here so late?

There's nothing wrong, I hope?"

Jessie shrank back against the door. She couldn't see the owner of the voice, but she knew exactly who it was. It was Mrs. Tweedie, their new next-door neighbor.

Mrs. Tweedie was a small, bustling woman with spiky gray hair, a pointed pink-tipped nose, and sharp blue eyes that darted around behind thick glasses. She reminded Jessie of a bird—a busy, curious, gossiping little bird. The Bins family, who used to live in Mrs. Tweedie's house, had done their best to ignore their neighbors at Blue Moon. Mrs. Tweedie did just the opposite.

She seemed to be fascinated by everything that happened next door. She was always popping in for one reason or another: to borrow something, or to ask advice, or to bring a box of cakes or cookies, saying she'd cooked too many for herself. She spent lots of time in her garden, keeping a close eye on all the comings and goings across the fence.

Granny said Mrs. Tweedie didn't have enough to do with her time. Rosemary said she was probably

14

lonely. Jessie had started to think she was just plain nosy.

And now Mrs. Tweedie had caught her sneaking out of the house at midnight! Jessie was desperately trying to think up a story to explain what she was doing when another voice floated from the garden at the front of the house.

"Oh, no, Louise. Flynn and I are just stargazing, that's all. We enjoy it at this time of year."

Granny! Jessie breathed a sigh of relief. So that was why the back door was unlocked. Granny was outside. Mrs. Tweedie had been talking to *her*, not to Jessie at all.

"How *interesting*!" exclaimed Mrs. Tweedie. "Was your late husband, the artist, keen on — um — star-gaping, too, Jessica?"

Granny laughed. "Oh, certainly," she said. "Robert liked nothing better! He could gape at the stars for hours at a time."

Jessie smothered a giggle as she crept down the back steps and onto the grass.

"I'm just back from the final Spring Fair meeting." Mrs. Tweedie was going on chattily. "Didn't

15

they keep us late? The Fair's on Saturday—well, you know that, of course, because it's at Jessie's school. Anyway, I heard that the organizers needed a few extra pairs of hands, so I went along to volunteer. That sort of thing's always a good way of getting to know people, isn't it?"

"Oh, yes," said Granny. Her voice was quite friendly, but Jessie could tell that she wished Mrs. Tweedie would leave her to stargaze in peace.

"Jessie's teacher, Lyn Stone, was there," Mrs. Tweedie babbled on. "She's been organizing the children's writing competition. What a *practical* young woman she is! But not what I'd call *friendly*, if you know what I mean."

You mean she wouldn't talk to you about me, you old busybody, Jessie thought. And for once she was grateful to Ms. Stone.

"That's nice," Granny murmured vaguely. "Well, Louise, don't let me keep you. . . ."

Jessie edged quietly into the trees and ran down to the high, clipped hedge that surrounded the secret garden. She hurried through the door in the hedge, and ran straight into Giff, who was waiting just inside.

With a little squeal, Giff bounced backward and fell flat on the grass.

"Oh, Giff, I'm so sorry!" Jessie whispered, crouching beside him and pulling him back to his feet. "Now, quickly, tell me what happened!"

"I bumped my head," Giff mumbled. "You knocked me over!" He swayed. Jessie held his arm firmly.

"I don't mean what happened just now," she whispered. "I mean—you said you were in some sort of trouble. What trouble?"

Giff blinked in a dazed sort of way. Then he slowly raised his hand to his bulging jacket pocket and an expression of horror dawned on his face.

"Oh dear, oh dear!" he moaned. "We have to hurry!" And before Jessie could move or say a word, he shouted, "Open!"

There was a sighing, whispering sound and a rush of cool wind. Jessie's skin began to tingle. Her hair flew around her head in a golden red cloud.

"N-no!" she stammered. "No, no, Giff, I can't—"

But it was too late. Already the secret garden had disappeared and mist was swirling around Jessie's face. A moment later she felt pebbles beneath her feet and smelled warm, sweet air. She and Giff were in the Realm.

"There!" squealed a familiar voice. "There he is, Maybelle! And Jessie's with him!"

The mist cleared from Jessie's eyes. She and Giff were on the pebbly road that ran beside the tall, dark hedge that protected the Realm. The sky above them was like black velvet sprayed with huge, twinkling diamonds.

And there, standing in front of them on the road, were Maybelle and Patrice. Maybelle was swishing her white tail crossly and pawing the ground with one hoof. Small, plump Patrice had her hands on her hips. Both of them were glaring at Giff.

"Oh, no!" wailed Giff. He clapped his hands over his eyes.

Maybelle snorted. "Did you really think you could get away with this, you fool of an elf?" she snapped. "The drawer's empty, and you were the only one to go to Queen Helena's room tonight, to get that box of griffin treats! Everyone else was stargazing. Come on! Where is it?"

"It's there." Patrice sighed, pointing at Giff's bulging jacket pocket. "Oh, Giff, how could you *do* such a thing!"

Giff whimpered.

"Patrice—Maybelle—what's happening?" Jessie burst out in confusion. "What's Giff done?"

"*Done*?" fumed Maybelle. "Oh, nothing much. He's only stuffed the most precious thing in the Realm into his grubby pocket and run away. He's only made off with Queen Helena's Star Cloak, the night before Wish Night, that's all!"

"I didn't make off with the Star Cloak!" Giff wailed, taking his hands away from his eyes. "I just—borrowed it. I was going to bring it back when . . . when . . ."

"I knew it!" exclaimed Patrice. "I just *knew* you'd taken it to show Jessie. When we discovered it was missing, Maybelle and I rushed straight here. Oh!" She fanned her hot face with her hand. "I'm so relieved we found you! You're just very lucky that no one knows about this but us. All right—give it to me."

She held out her small, brown hand. But Giff clutched at his pocket, shrank back against Jessie, and shook his head.

"Giff!" thundered Maybelle. "Give—the Star Cloak—to—Patrice!"

Giff just kept shaking his head. Jessie could feel him trembling. She put her arm around his quivering shoulders and frowned. Something was very wrong here, and she had a horrible feeling that she knew what it was.

# the cloak

"You didn't really take the Star Cloak just to show me, did you, Giff?" Jessie asked gently.

"No," Giff moaned. "I wanted . . . I wanted you to come with me, Jessie. I was too scared to go on my own."

"What are you babbling about?" demanded Maybelle. "Too scared to go *where* on your own?"

Patrice wasn't listening. Her small black eyes were fixed on Giff's hands, which were still clutched protectively over his pocket. *Patrice suspects what I suspect*, Jessie thought, and her heart sank.

"Why won't you give me the Star Cloak, Giff?" Patrice asked in a level voice.

Giff's eyes widened in terror.

"Something awful's happened," Patrice went on. "I feel it in my bones. Come on, Giff, you might as well tell us. The Cloak's been damaged, hasn't it?"

"What?" roared Maybelle. *"Damaged!"*

Giff suddenly went limp. His hands dropped to his sides. His ears drooped miserably. "It wasn't my fault," he whispered. "I found the griffin treats in a drawer, and as I was getting them out, I pulled another drawer open by mistake. The Star Cloak was there, in its bag. And I—I just thought I'd have a peep at it. Just a tiny peep, Patrice. But the Cloak was rolled up so tightly that I couldn't really see it. So . . . so . . ."

"So you took it out of the bag," Patrice said grimly. "You unrolled it. And then—"

Giff burst into tears. "I didn't mean it to happen!" He sobbed. "I was just looking. It was so beautiful! It swirled around me like tingly spiderwebs. I don't know how my foot got caught in it.

But somehow it did, and I got all tangled up, and I fell over, and there was this awful, tearing sound and—"

"Don't say any more," said Maybelle, closing her eyes. She tossed her head at Patrice. "Get it," she ordered. "We may as well know the worst."

Patrice pulled a small black velvet bag from Giff's jacket pocket. Giff sobbed even harder, but made no move to stop her.

Jessie watched, fascinated, as Patrice untied the bag's silver drawstrings, pulled the bag open, and slowly drew out a little roll of shimmering, pale blue cloth.

But that can't be the Cloak, Jessie thought. It's much too small. Then she gasped as Patrice held the roll high and shook it out.

The Star Cloak billowed free, floating in the sweet night air. It sparkled like blue and silver starlight, delicate as a fairy's wing, light as spun gossamer, glimmering with magic.

But right in the center of the back, running almost to the hem, was an ugly, gaping tear. Even as the friends watched, a few sparkling threads drifted away from the tear and floated toward the ground.

Patrice drew a sharp breath. Maybelle drew her lips back from her teeth. Giff buried his face in his hands. "I put the Cloak on and wished the tear would go away," he wailed. "But it didn't work. The tear just got bigger!"

"I can't believe this has happened," Patrice murmured at last. "This Cloak was new last year. It's not due to be replaced till the next blue moon — and that's — that's forty-nine years from now!" She was very pale. Her plump hands trembled as she gently rolled up the Cloak again. "Oh, how can Queen Helena wear the Cloak like this?"

"She can't!" Maybelle said shortly. "The threads won't stay in place now that they're torn, you know that, Patrice. If Queen Helena wears the Cloak tomorrow night, there'll be nothing left of it by dawn. No, there's nothing to be done. Wish Night will have to be canceled."

"But crowds from the farthest parts of the Realm are already on their way!" cried Patrice. "By the time we can spread the word, most of them will have arrived at the palace. And all so excited, in their best clothes, with their wishes ready—"

Giff gave an agonized, muffled groan.

"But surely the whole of Wish Night doesn't have to be canceled just because the Star Cloak is torn!" Jessie exclaimed. "Surely Queen Helena has other beautiful clothes she could wear."

As soon as the words left her mouth she realized she'd said something stupid. Patrice, Maybelle, and even Giff were staring at her in astonishment.

"The Star Cloak *is* Wish Night, dearie," Patrice said gently after a moment. "Didn't you know? It's the Star Cloak's magic that makes the stars fall. If Queen Helena doesn't wear it . . . well, nothing will happen at all."

"Oh," said Jessie weakly. "I didn't realize." For the first time, she understood that Giff had been speaking the truth when he'd said he was in the worst trouble ever.

"No point in standing here talking," Maybelle muttered. "We'd better go and tell Queen Helena."

"No!" wailed Giff, throwing himself on the ground. "No, no, no, no, no! You can't tell *anyone*! And Wish Night *can't* be canceled. Everyone will blame me! Everyone will hate me! No one will ever speak to me again!"

"Oh, I daresay they'll forgive you eventually," Maybelle said curtly. "In a hundred years or so." She tossed her mane. "If you live that long," she added. "Which I doubt, if the griffins get to hear of this."

Giff burst into tears again.

Jessie felt so sorry for him. It had been very wrong of him to touch the Star Cloak. But the results had been so terrible that surely he'd been punished enough. He'd run to her for help—but so far she'd done nothing for him at all.

Then she remembered something he'd said. "Giff," she murmured. "You said you wanted me to go somewhere with you—somewhere you were afraid to go alone. Where was that?"

"S-Stardust Mountain." Giff sobbed. "That's w-where the Star Cloak was made. The star fairies there could mend it; I know they could. I thought — I thought if we could get there and back by tomorrow morning, no one would ever have to know. But now —"

"Stardust Mountain indeed!" snorted Maybelle. "Are you out of your mind? Even if the star fairies didn't sting you to death when they saw what you'd done to a Star Cloak that took them *fifty years* to make, how did you think you and Jessie could get to the Mountain and back in a single night?"

Giff took a shuddering breath. "I thought we could use the Cloak," he said. "I thought we could put it around us, very carefully, and wish. Queen Helena told me that whoever wears the Cloak can make wishes anytime, not just on Wish Night. All you have to do is wish for the thing you want most in the world. The wish has to be possible, and there have to be stars in the sky. Going to Star Mountain *is* possible, and there are lots of stars tonight."

There was a short silence. Then Patrice and Maybelle glanced at each other.

"It could work, you know," Patrice said slowly.

"And it would solve everything."

"Have you ever seen a star fairy in a temper, Patrice?" Maybelle retorted.

Patrice frowned. "Very nasty," she agreed. "But maybe . . ."

She turned to Jessie, who was staring at them, wide-eyed. "It's like this, dearie," she said carefully. "The fairies on Stardust Mountain are a bit touchy, if you know what I mean."

"A *bit* touchy?" snorted Maybelle.

"They have to be approached in just the right way or there's trouble," Patrice went on, flapping a hand at Maybelle to quiet her. "Not that they're *bad*, you understand. But they're very secretive, and they don't like strangers coming to the Mountain. I was thinking that if *you* were with us, Jessie, they might be so interested to meet you that they'd keep their tempers and fix the Cloak for us, too."

"That's what *I* thought!" Giff snuffled, wiping his eyes and climbing to his feet. "That's why I wanted Jessie to come with me."

Patrice frowned at him. "How you could even

*think* of taking Jessie to Stardust Mountain with only you to look after her, I do not know!" she snapped. "It's very lucky we caught you in time. If we go, we'll all go together."

"And it had better be soon," muttered Maybelle, glancing at the sky. "The night's not getting any younger. What do you say, Jessie? Will you come with us?"

Jessie hesitated. If she agreed to go to Stardust Mountain, she'd be away from home all night. She wouldn't get any sleep at all!

She thought of school tomorrow, and Ms. Stone. Then she looked at Giff's tear-stained face and pleading eyes and knew that there was only one choice she could make. "Of course I'll go with you," she said warmly. "As long as I can be back by the time Mum gets home from work in the morning, I'd be happy to help."

# stardust mountain

"We'll be back from Stardust Mountain long before your mother gets home, Jessie," said Patrice, patting Jessie's arm. "We'll have to be, whatever happens. It would be terribly dangerous to have a Star Cloak outdoors after dawn."

"One ray of sunlight will destroy it," Maybelle explained, seeing Jessie's confused expression. "Well, what would you expect? It *is* made of woven stardust and moonbeams."

Jessie's jaw dropped.

"I thought you knew, dearie!" exclaimed Patrice. "The star fairy workers spin dust from falling stars with beams from the blue moon to make the threads. Then they weave the threads together to make the cloth. That's why the Cloak's so magic, and so precious. The black velvet bag gives it some protection, of course, but we wouldn't want to take any risks."

"We'd better get moving, then, hadn't we?" said Maybelle bossily. "Now, Jessie, you'll wear the Cloak, because you're the tallest—"

"And, besides, it's only right!" Patrice put in. "Jessie *is* Queen Jessica's granddaughter."

Maybelle rolled her eyes. "That, too," she said. "Giff, you stand beside Jessie. When the Cloak's in place, Patrice can get on the other side, and I'll stand in front. We all have to be covered completely before we wish, and while we're traveling. When I give the signal, we all think, 'I wish I were with the fairies on Stardust Mountain,' and really mean it. Is that understood?"

"Of course it's understood, Maybelle!" snapped Patrice as she handed the black velvet bag to Jessie and began unrolling the Star Cloak once more. "We're not silly."

"Some of us are," said Maybelle darkly, shooting a glance at Giff.

Jessie tucked the bag into her pocket and held out her arm. Giff shot to her side and snuggled against her. Patrice draped the floating blue folds of the Cloak around both of them.

Jessie shivered. The Cloak was as light as air, but she could feel a cool tingling all over her body, right through her clothes. She could hear Giff's teeth chattering.

"It's cold!" Giff whimpered.

"Yes, Queen Helena always says that," said Patrice as she stood on her toes and started tying the Cloak's silver strings at Jessie's neck. "And I remember her dear mother saying it before her. Ah, well. Magic isn't always comfortable."

"I can hear something!" Maybelle said sharply.

Patrice stiffened, listening intently. "Someone's coming along the road!" she whispered. "From the direction of the palace, too. It sounds like . . . Oh, Maybelle, it sounds like—"

"What?" cried Giff in panic from beneath the Cloak.

"It sounds like a troop of guards," Maybelle hissed. "Get those strings tied, Patrice!"

"I'm trying!" panted Patrice, fumbling with the silver strings. "You know how slippery they are. And if they aren't tied properly we'll lose the Cloak on the way. Oh, paddywinks and sossle-bones! I keep losing my grip."

"This is a disaster!" Maybelle growled.

Now Jessie, too, could hear the marching feet coming toward them. She couldn't see anything, because of a bend in the road, but the sounds were becoming louder and louder. At any moment the troop would round the bend and see them.

"Hurry, Patrice!" she whispered.

"Troop—halt!" a guard yelled, and the marching feet stopped.

"That's Loris's voice," Maybelle muttered. "It must be something important for *his* troop to be sent out. They weren't on duty tonight. The last I saw of them they were stargazing with everyone else."

"You there!" they heard Loris roar. "You rabbits under that tree—yes, you, with the daisies behind your ears! Have you seen an elf come by here?"

Jessie's stomach turned over. She heard Giff whimper beneath the Cloak and pressed his hand comfortingly. Patrice grunted with effort as she wrestled with the silver strings.

"Well?" called Loris, more loudly.

"We 'aven't done nuffin'," a snuffly voice called back. "We 'aven't done nuffin', an' we don't know about nuffin'. 'Cept grass."

"An' daisies," a squeakier voice put in.

"An' daisies," the snuffly voice repeated loudly. "We don't know about nuffin' but grass and daisies."

"An' carrots," said the squeaky voice. "An' lettuce. An'—"

There was a loud chorus of snuffly, shushing sounds.

"It's no good asking them anything, Loris," snapped a guard's voice. "They've got nothing but fluff between the ears."

"That's rude, that is!" retorted the first rabbit. "We could report you for that!"

"We could report *you* for being deliberately unhelpful!" snapped Loris. "Have you seen an elf, or not?"

"Maybe we 'ave, and maybe we 'aven't," said the first rabbit, with a sniff. "Maybe 'e came runnin' down the road here, red in the face and puffin' like a walrus, with somefin' big stuffed in 'is pocket, and maybe 'e didn't. We'll never tell you lot, any'ow!"

"The silly thing has told them already!" hissed Patrice.

"Troop!" roared Loris at the same moment. "Quick march!"

"Oh, no!" squeaked Giff. "They're coming! They'll catch me! Oh! Oh! I wish we were in Stardust Mountain with the star fairies!"

Instantly Jessie's skin felt cold as ice. A blue light flamed before her eyes. She heard Patrice scream. Then everything went dark.

When she woke, she was shivering. She had no idea how much time had passed. She opened her eyes and saw tiny flashing lights swirling around her. An angry humming filled her ears. Quickly she shut her eyes again.

Slowly her mind began working. She felt the cool, tingling folds of the Star Cloak wrapped around her. She remembered that Giff had panicked and wished them to Stardust Mountain, leaving Patrice and Maybelle behind. But where was Giff now? She couldn't feel him, or hear him. All she could hear was that strange buzzing sound . . .

She forced her eyes open again. She was lying on her back. Tiny lights were still whirling above her. Beyond them were other lights—thousands of stars twinkling in the night sky. They looked so close that Jessie felt she could touch them if she stretched out her hand.

But the whirling lights were even closer. They were swooping low over her upturned face, buzzing like a swarm of bees. And then Jessie saw that they weren't lights, but tiny fairies whose pale skin glowed and sparkled.

There were hundreds of them. They had long, silky, pale blue hair, and their robes were silver, blue, and mauve. Their wings were whirring so fast that they made a humming sound. Their pointed faces did not look friendly.

The star fairies, Jessie thought fearfully.

The fairies at the front of the swarm were larger than the rest. They were scowling. Their long, white fingers, tipped with nails as sharp as needles, were jabbing the air. "Who are you, human girl?" they were crying in tiny, buzzing voices. "Why have you come to our Mountain? How did you dare to use the Star Cloak? Explain! Explain! Explain!"

Jessie cleared her throat. "I am Jessie, granddaughter of Jessica, the Realm's true queen," she managed to say. "I have come to ask you—"

"Jessie!" some of the smaller fairies cried excitedly. "Queen Helena told us of Jessie! Jessie saved the Realm last year, at the time of the blue moon!"

Chattering, they tried to press forward, but the larger fairies at the front held them back. Jessie decided that the larger fairies must be the swarm's soldiers. Their fierce expressions had not changed, and they still held their thornlike nails at the ready.

"She *says* she is Jessie, but she offers us no proof," one of them droned. "I think she lies! Why would the granddaughter of Queen Jessica come here without warning, and with no royal guards to

40

protect her? And why would Queen Helena let the Star Cloak out of her sight, the night before Wish Night?"

"Warrior Flash is right," another said. "We must think of this further."

"We do not need to think further!" buzzed the fierce fairy called Flash, jabbing at Jessie with her pointed nails. "We should sting her, sting her until she tells the truth!"

"No!" Jessie cried desperately. "I really *am* Jessie, I am! Ask Giff—the elf who came with me. He'll tell you I'm not lying!"

"No one came with you," snapped Flash, her frown deepening. "What trick are you playing?"

Jessie felt a stab of fear. Giff must have fallen from under the Star Cloak as they reached Stardust Mountain. He was lost somewhere on the Mountain, and she was here alone.

"She is an invader!" cried Flash. "Warriors, attack!"

And instantly all the soldier fairies dived straight at Jessie, their needle-sharp nails glinting in the light.

41

# flash and gleam

Jessie screamed and flung her arms over her face. Dimly she heard her charm bracelet jingling on her wrist. She thought of her mother, of Granny, of Giff, Patrice, Maybelle, Queen Helena. They can't help me, she thought in terror. No one can help me. . . .

Then she realized that the angry buzzing had stopped. It had changed to a low humming. And the star fairies had not touched her.

Cautiously she moved her arms a little, and opened her eyes. She saw that the swarm was circling over her charm bracelet.

"You see!" one of the smaller fairies cried. "She *is* Jessie! She wears the golden bracelet, hung with Realm gifts, just as Queen Helena told us. It is the proof! The proof!"

The humming swarm drew back until it was hovering at a respectful distance. The warriors put their hands behind their backs, as if to show they were no longer a threat.

Weak with relief, Jessie sat up. She saw that she was on a high mountaintop, surrounded by big rocks and clusters of sweet-smelling plants. Huge stars blazed above her, and everything was bathed in a strange, magical light. Wondering where the light was coming from, Jessie glanced behind her. There, not far above where she was sitting, was the very tip of the Mountain. Cool, white light was streaming from it, flooding the rocks below.

Jessie shivered and huddled farther into the folds of the Star Cloak. But the slippery, magic cloth did not warm her any more than the light did.

The star fairies had been talking seriously to one another. Now they fell silent, and one lonely figure flew forward. As it came closer, Jessie saw that it was the soldier fairy, Warrior Flash.

"We beg your pardon, Jessie," said Flash stiffly. "The fault was mine, for I ordered the attack. I await my punishment. My life is yours to take."

"Oh . . . no!" Jessie exclaimed. "I don't want to hurt you."

A great buzzing rose from the listening swarm. There was a whir of wings, and the next moment, the smaller fairies were dancing in the air in front of Jessie, their faces bright with relief. She held out her hands to them and dozens of them landed on her fingers, chattering and laughing. But the soldiers kept their distance, looking wary and puzzled.

"I thank you for sparing me," Flash said slowly. "I do not understand your reasons, however. You do not seem to be a weakling."

"Clearly Jessie is no weakling," one of the other soldier fairies agreed. "She showed courage when we attacked. She could have used the Star Cloak to escape us, but she did not. Her mission here must be of great importance."

Jessie looked up quickly. Of course! she thought. I'm wearing the Star Cloak, so I could have just wished myself away from here. I was just so confused and frightened that I completely forgot!

She opened her mouth to say this, then changed her mind. The star fairy warriors seemed to value strength and courage above everything else. It would be best not to admit to any weakness.

She crawled to her feet. The little fairies in her hands flew upward in a shining cloud. She felt the cool folds of the Star Cloak float around her and took a deep breath. "My mission *is* important," she said, keeping her voice as calm and level as she could. "I'm afraid the Cloak is damaged." She turned around, so that the fairies could see the ragged tear.

A loud, horrified buzzing rose from the swarm. Then Jessie felt the breeze of whirring wings, and her spine tingled as hundreds of tiny hands touched the damaged Cloak.

"Take it off! Take it off!" the fairies cried

frantically. "Every moment more threads drift free, and the damage grows worse!"

Jessie felt for the silver strings and untied them. The Cloak slipped from her shoulders. She turned and saw it being swept away through the air, completely covered by the smaller fairies and surrounded by the warriors. Only Flash remained, hovering before her.

"Where are they taking it?" Jessie asked anxiously.

"To the Cavern," said Flash sternly, pointing over Jessie's head to the glowing tip of the Mountain. "There the Oldest One will decide if mending is possible. Did *you* damage the Star Cloak?"

"No," Jessie said, very glad that it was the truth.

"Then name the culprit!" Flash buzzed. "The enemy who tore the Cloak must be found and punished."

"There is no enemy," exclaimed Jessie. "It was an accident."

Flash's sharp eyes narrowed. "When you arrived, you said that an elf called Giff was with you," she said coldly. "But you were alone. I think this Giff damaged the Cloak, then was too afraid to show his face here, because he knew what we would do. No doubt he is hiding somewhere on the Mountain. When the other warriors return, we will begin the hunt for him."

Filled with dismay, Jessie turned away so Flash couldn't see her face. But she knew it was too late. The fairy had already guessed part of the truth, and now Giff was in terrible danger.

I have to stop them from going after him, Jessie thought. I have to give him time to get away from the Mountain. Even if he's captured by the palace guards, that would be much better than being caught by the star fairies.

"I don't think you should go hunting anyone, Flash," she said aloud. "You and the others should stay here to protect the Cloak."

There was silence for a moment. Jessie didn't turn around. Again she looked up at the tip of the Mountain. Now she could see that the light she had noticed before was streaming from the mouth of a huge cave. The light flowed over her, beautiful but cold, and suddenly she longed for the sun.

At last Flash spoke again. "I know that for some reason you want to save this elf from the punishment he deserves," she said. "But still, what you say is true. The Cloak must be guarded, so the search must wait. There is no great hurry, anyway. Strangers lost on the Mountain never escape it without help. There are too many cliffs and holes for that."

Jessie thought of poor Giff, lost and alone. He was never very brave at any time. What must he be feeling now? Don't panic, Giff, she told him in her mind. Don't do anything silly or dangerous. The moment I get the Star Cloak back, I'll wish I was with you. Then I'll wish us both back to the palace.

Her heart thudded as she saw three glowing specks shoot from the cavern's mouth and hurtle down toward them. Three of the soldier fairies were returning. What news would they bring? What if they said the Star Cloak was beyond repair? What if they said it would take days, or even weeks, to mend?

The three newcomers stopped directly in front of her. "The news is good," said the largest of the three. "The Cloak can be mended. The work has already begun. It will take many hours, but will be finished before the last star has faded from the sky."

A wave of relief flowed over Jessie. "Oh, I'm so glad!" she cried. "So *glad*!"

The soldier fairy nodded. "We, too, are glad," he said gravely. "The Oldest One has invited you to wait in the Cavern while —"

"None but the star fairies may enter the Cavern, Warrior Gleam," Flash snapped. "Even Queen Helena and Princess Christie remained outside when they came a year ago to accept the new Cloak. You must be mistaken."

Gleam calmly shook his head. "I am not mistaken," he said. "The Oldest One reminds us that our mountaintop is too cold for Folk to remain on for long without harm. The same is true of humans. The Oldest One does not want Jessie to become ill, for who then would return the Cloak to the Queen?"

Flash thought for a moment, then nodded. "Follow!" she ordered Jessie. Then she began to fly upward, a floating glimmer of light. Gleam and the other fairies went with her, their long, fine hair drifting around their heads in pale blue clouds. They looked so beautiful, and so delicate, it was hard to believe that they could harm anyone—or want to.

It just goes to show that you can't judge people by what they look like, Jessie thought, climbing after her guides. If it hadn't been for the charm bracelet, they would have stung me to death without a shred of pity.

As they drew closer to the tip of the Mountain, the humming sound grew louder, the light grew brighter, and the magic in the air became so strong that Jessie's skin was prickling with it. She began to climb faster.

Flash, Gleam, and their companions reached the cave and hovered at the entrance, almost invisible in the radiant glow. Jessie arrived at their side, panting, and only then realized that all the other star fairy warriors were at the Cavern's mouth, too. The light was filled with hundreds of small, flying figures with fierce faces and needle-sharp nails.

"We will enter," Flash said loudly. "It is the will of the Oldest One."

The warrior fairies moved aside, putting their hands behind their backs to show that they would not strike.

Her heart pounding, her eyes watering in the light, Jessie moved through the entrance, and into the Cavern.

CHAPTER SIX

# The Cavern

The Cavern was huge and echoing. Its corners were dim, but its center was glowing with light. Hundreds of star fairies were gathered there, working on the damaged Star Cloak, which floated, glittering, a little way off the floor.

Fairies were clustered thickly along both sides of the long, ragged tear, their wings humming, their fingers flying as they wove loose threads together. Other fairies, their hands filled with shining blue and silver, were flying up and down along the center of the tear, dropping new threads to workers who needed them.

"Are those threads really made of stardust and moonbeams?" Jessie whispered.

"Of course," said Gleam, who was flying just in front of her. "They have been spun for the next Star Cloak, but the Oldest One has ordered that as many as are needed can be used for the mending."

"You should not speak," muttered Flash, from Jessie's other side. "The workers must not be disturbed. We will take Jessie to the rest chamber, Warrior Gleam. She will sleep there, and cause no trouble."

"The Oldest One has asked to see her, Warrior Flash," said Gleam. "The Oldest One is curious to see the granddaughter of Queen Jessica."

Flash buzzed sullenly, but did not argue. This fairy they call the Oldest One must be their leader, Jessie thought. She felt nervous as she followed the two soldier fairies around the mass of working fairies and into the most brilliant part of the light.

There, a chair of woven grass hung high above the ground, suspended by sparkling threads. In the chair, watching the work being done below, sat the most ancient fairy Jessie had ever seen. Her flowing hair was silver-white. Her tiny face and hands looked almost transparent, as if they were made of pure light. But her robes were a deep, rich blue, and her gray eyes were filled with interest as she looked up and caught sight of Jessie.

Jessie bowed awkwardly, too nervous to speak.

"You look very like your grandmother," the old fairy said in a harsh, cracked voice. "It is good to see you here, though what you brought with you gave us pain."

Her eyes moved from Jessie's face down to the damaged Star Cloak. Suddenly she frowned. "Worker Glitter!" she called sharply. "You have missed a thread! Undo your work and begin again!"

A small fairy in blue jumped, ducked her head, and began plucking nervously at a group of threads so tiny that Jessie couldn't even see them.

The Oldest One sighed. "The young workers need watching every moment," she said. "The mending must be done speedily, that is true, but still it must be done well. This Star Cloak must last through the coming Wish Night, and forty-eight other Wish Nights, too, before a new Cloak can be ready to replace it."

"So—so Star Cloaks really *do* take fifty whole years to make?" stammered Jessie, finding her voice at last. "Is that because there's only a blue moon once every fifty years?"

"No," said the Oldest One, without taking her eyes off the workers. "We can always gather more than enough blue moonbeams to store for our purposes. Stardust is another matter." She moved restlessly in her chair. "It takes a great deal of stardust to make a Star Cloak. It is hard to gather as much as we need, even in fifty years."

"How do you gather it?" Jessie asked, fascinated. Flash buzzed angrily in her ear, and even Gleam made an uncomfortable sound, but the Oldest One only smiled.

"You are as full of questions as your grandmother was when she visited us," she said. "And I will answer you, just as I answered her, long ago."

She pointed upward. Jessie looked up and was startled to see, high above her, a vast gap in the

Cavern roof. Beyond the gap was the brilliance of the night sky.

"During the day, when we sleep, the sky window is covered, to protect our work," the old fairy explained. "But at night it is always open, to catch the dust of any star that falls above our Mountain. The dust sweeps in like shining snow, attracted by the stardust we already have. And we gather it, gather it as fast as we can, in silken bags, and add it to our store."

Jessie thought for a moment. "Stars don't fall very often, except on Wish Night," she said slowly. "So Wish Night must be a very important night for you, every year."

"*Important?*" The Oldest One gave a harsh, buzzing laugh that had little humor in it. "You could say that! Why do you think we agreed to put aside our work to mend the damaged Cloak so quickly?"

She frowned, tapping her tiny fingers, waiting for an answer.

"So . . . so that Wish Night won't have to be canceled," said Jessie uncertainly. "So that the stars will still fall. And so you—"

"So we will survive!" snapped the Oldest One. "If we miss even one Wish Night, we will not have enough stardust to finish the new Star Cloak by the time the old Cloak fades at the next blue moon. The magic line will be broken. There will be no new Star Cloak. There will be no more Wish Nights."

Her eyes darkened. Her hands clenched into fists. "And if the Star Cloaks end, so does the star fairies' purpose," she said. "Our work is our life. If the Star Cloaks end, we, too, will fade away."

Jessie gasped in horror.

"Leave me now," the Oldest One said abruptly. "Your likeness to your grandmother made me show weakness. I have told you too many of our secrets already. Keep them to yourself, if you value our friendship."

Flash and Gleam tweaked Jessie's hair, urging her away. Jessie stumbled back, bowed again to the Oldest One, then followed the two fairies as they led her to a shadowy corner of the Cavern.

She was horrified by what she had heard. Patrice, Maybelle, and Giff don't know about this, she thought. They were only worried about the Realm people being disappointed if Wish Night were canceled. They don't realize that missing one Wish Night would mean the end of the Star Cloaks, and the star fairies, too.

She remembered the Oldest One's last, mumbled words. *I have told you too many of our secrets already. . . .*

The star fairies hate to admit to any weakness, Jessie thought. They don't trust anyone to understand them, so they've always kept their troubles secret. I might be the only person in the Realm—except maybe Queen Helena—to know how important every Wish Night is to them.

"You can wait in here." Flash's sharp voice cut through Jessie's thoughts. She looked up and saw that her guides were hovering in front of an archway that led into another, smaller cave.

"I am not sure that the workers' rest chamber is the best place for Jessie to wait, Warrior Flash," Gleam said quietly. "Jessie is not even of the Folk. She is human."

"No lasting harm will come to her, Warrior

Gleam!" Flash snapped. "And I must be certain that she will not find a way to creep out of the Cavern to find Giff the elf and help him to escape. Leave us now. You are needed at the entrance."

Gleam hesitated, his face creased in concern. Then he bowed his head and flew quickly away.

Jessie looked anxiously into the dimness beyond the archway. She couldn't see anything. "Couldn't I just wait here, at the side of the Cavern?" she asked in a low voice. "I wouldn't try to creep out, I promise. I've got no idea where Giff is. I couldn't find him, even if I tried!"

"You must wait in the rest chamber," Flash said harshly. "We will call you when the Cloak is ready."

Jessie knew it would be useless to argue anymore. Nervously, wishing she knew why Gleam had been so worried, she moved into the cave. It was warmer than the great Cavern had been, and the air was heavy with a tangy scent that reminded Jessie of the rosemary bushes in the secret garden.

Gradually her eyes grew used to the dimness and she saw that thick couches of dried leaves lined the cave walls. That's where the perfume's coming from, she thought. The couches. The leaves . . .

She hadn't felt sleepy before, but suddenly her eyelids felt very heavy—so heavy that she could hardly keep them open. Almost without noticing what she was doing, she moved to the nearest couch and lay down. The leaves cushioned her in rustling, fragrant softness.

Something in this cave makes you sleep, she realized hazily. The scent of the leaves, maybe. Or just magic. That's why Flash wanted me here. And that's why Gleam was worried. This place is meant for star fairies, not for Folk, or humans. That's why . . .

But she never finished the thought. Her eyes closed, and in seconds she was fast asleep.

# CHAPTER SEVEN

# Dreams

Jessie was dreaming of the secret garden. The rosemary bushes were humming with bees. The tall, green hedge seemed to keep the whole world out. She felt wonderfully happy and peaceful.

The humming of the bees grew louder, and suddenly there was a sharp buzz right beside her ear. One of the bees had come too close. She tried to brush it away. The buzzing didn't stop. And now it was starting to sound like a voice—a tiny voice, calling her anxiously.

Jessie frowned. She didn't want to listen to the voice. She didn't want to leave the secret garden where she felt so happy and safe.

"I *told* you it was dangerous to leave her here, Warrior Flash!" the little voice said. "The resting magic is too strong for humans."

"Jessie, *get up*!" raged another voice, and Jessie felt her hair being pulled painfully. She forced her eyes open. Through a sleepy haze she saw two small, shining figures hovering in front of her. She crawled to her feet and stood swaying and blinking in confusion.

"Jessie, the Cloak is ready, but the stars are fading," buzzed the second voice. "Come quickly!"

Star fairies, Jessie thought dreamily. They want me to go with them. But I don't want to. I want to go back to the secret garden.

Tiny hands tugged at her hair again. Slowly it came to Jessie that the little creatures wouldn't leave her alone until she'd done what they wanted her to do. She followed them out of the dimness and into a huge cavern that glowed with light and echoed with a humming sound.

I've been here before, Jessie thought, but she couldn't remember when or why. She stumbled after her guides till she stood below a great gap in the cavern roof. Through the gap she could see a single star glimmering faintly in a pale gray sky. It looked very far away—far away, and cold. She remembered the light and warmth of the secret garden. That was better, she thought. Much better . . .

"Put on the Cloak, Jessie!" an old, cracked voice ordered. "Make haste! Only one star remains. When it fades, it will be too late to wish, and the Cloak will not be returned in time. Workers, help her!"

Jessie felt something cool and tingling float onto her shoulders. She heard the whirring of wings, and felt tiny, clever fingers fastening strings at her neck. Soon, she thought, her eyelids drooping. Soon . . .

"Beware, Oldest One!" a voice called urgently. "The girl is still half asleep. She—"

"Be silent, Warrior Gleam!" snapped the old voice. "There is no time! The Cloak is tied, Jessie. Make your wish and go!"

At last, Jessie thought drowsily. She let her eyes close, and wished with all her heart that she was back in the secret garden.

❋ ❋ ❋

Jessie woke to the sound of birds calling. She lay
still for a moment, eyes closed, enjoying the
memory of the lovely dream she'd just had. She'd
been in the secret garden, perfectly happy. Someone
had made her leave it, but then she'd been able to
return. It had been wonderful.

She shivered, and slowly realized that she was
cold, and that the softness beneath her cheek was
damp. She opened her eyes and stared around her
in confusion. She really *was* in the secret garden,
lying on the grass in the shadow of the tall hedge.
How had this happened?

And suddenly memory flooded back. The Star
Cloak! She'd taken the Star Cloak to be mended,
but . . . Panic-stricken, she touched the cool folds
of the Star Cloak, still wrapped around her. She
sat bolt upright and looked wildly up at the sky. It
arched over her, blue with just a trace of white
cloud. And the sun . . . the sun!

A golden pool of sunlight was lying in the
entrance to the secret garden. The pool was grow-
ing by the moment, moving toward her as the sun

climbed higher in the sky. It had nearly reached her — nearly reached the Star Cloak.

Maybelle's voice echoed in her mind. *One ray of sunlight will destroy it. One ray of sunlight will . . .*

Frantically Jessie tore at the silver strings that tied the Cloak. They slipped beneath her fingers. The sunlight was stealing closer. She gathered the Cloak around her and scrambled back. Forcing herself to be calm, she pulled at the strings again, and this time managed to untie them.

She stood up and pulled the Cloak from her shoulders. It floated in her hands, drifting in the air like a spiderweb. The sunlight had almost reached her feet. She backed away from it, frantically rolling the folds of the Cloak into a tight package. Turning her back to the sunlight, she felt in her pocket for the black velvet bag, hoping desperately that she had not lost it.

The bag was there. Jessie pulled it out and stuffed the Star Cloak inside. She forced the bag deep into her pocket again, and breathed a sigh of relief. The Cloak was safe. Now all she had to do was go through the Door to the realm and return it to the palace.

"Jessie! What on earth are you doing out here so early?"

Jessie jumped violently and spun around, covering her bulging pocket with her hands. Her mother was standing at the entrance to the secret garden. She was wearing an overcoat over her nurse's uniform and looked very tired.

"Oh—hi, Mum," Jessie said weakly. "You're home!"

"And what a welcome I got!" Rosemary said, shaking her head and smiling. "No tea in the pot, Granny fast asleep, and you gone." She beckoned. "Don't just stand there, Jessie! You should be getting ready for school."

Jessie found her voice at last. "I—I'll come in a minute, Mum," she said.

"Oh no," said Rosemary firmly. "If I leave you, you'll start daydreaming again."

"Mum, just a few more minutes," Jessie pleaded. "I promise I'll—"

"Jessie, it's been a long night," her mother said, sighing. "Just come, will you?"

Jessie knew there was no point in arguing. What am I going to do? she thought desperately as she followed her mother out of the secret garden and up to the house. I've got to tell someone about poor Giff. And I've got to get the Cloak back to Queen Helena! Oh, why did I wish myself back here, instead of to the palace? How could I have been so stupid?

She clenched her fists, and forced herself to be calm. She knew that panic wouldn't help. If I get changed and have breakfast really quickly, maybe Mum will stop worrying about me and I'll be able to slip down to the secret garden again, she thought. If that doesn't work, I'll hide the Star Cloak somewhere and tell Granny about it. She doesn't go to the Realm very often, but she'd do it for an emergency like this.

She realized that she'd reached the back steps, and that Rosemary was opening the door and going into the kitchen. Jessie was suddenly very aware of the big bulge the Star Cloak made in her pocket. So far her mother hadn't noticed it, but as soon as they were inside she'd see it and ask about it for sure.

Panic started to rise in Jessie all over again. Then she saw a basket of clothes just inside the back door. Rosemary had her back turned, and was pulling off her coat. Quickly Jessie dragged the Star Cloak bag out of her pocket and stuffed it deep into the basket.

Just in time. Rosemary turned around. "You need a haircut, Jessie," she murmured, brushing the hair out of Jessie's eyes. Her hand dropped to Jessie's shoulder and she drew back, frowning in concern. "You're all damp!" she exclaimed, patting Jessie's clothes. "Don't tell me you've been lying on the wet grass? Oh, Jessie, what am I going to do with you? Go and get out of those things straight-away. And you'd better have a quick shower to warm yourself up. You're freezing!"

Jessie scuttled off to her room and grabbed her school clothes. As she hurried to the bathroom, she heard her mother talking to someone. Who could be visiting this early? She listened curiously, then recognized the second voice. It was Mrs. Tweedie from next door.

She's made some excuse to come in, Jessie

thought crossly, moving quickly on to the bathroom. I'll bet she's dying to ask Mum about Granny watching the stars in the middle of the night.

She showered and changed in record time, and in ten minutes she was back in the kitchen. Her mother, who was sitting at the table, drinking tea, raised her eyebrows in surprise. "That was quick," she said.

Jessie forced a smile and nodded. She put some cereal into a bowl and grabbed a spoon. Then she sat down at the table with her mother and reached for the milk jug. "What did Mrs. Tweedie want, Mum?" she asked, for something to say.

Rosemary sighed. "Apparently she's got herself involved in the Spring Fair. She came to pick up the stuff we're giving to the secondhand clothes stall. She said the organizers were going to put prices on everything in the school assembly hall today. Luckily I had everything packed ready in that old laundry basket, so . . ."

Jessie went cold. The jug tipped sideways, and milk sloshed onto the table. She could hear her mother exclaiming, but she couldn't hear the words.

Then she felt Rosemary taking the jug from her, and putting a cool hand on her forehead.

"Jessie, what's wrong? You're pale as a ghost!"

"I've—only got a bit of a headache," Jessie managed to say. "I'm all right."

But she wasn't all right. There was a roaring in her ears. Her mind had gone numb. She was staring across the table at the back door—at the place where the basket of clothes had stood.

The basket had gone. And the Star Cloak had gone with it.

# CHAPTER EIGHT

# The Longest Day

Jessie could hardly remember the next twenty minutes. There were just flashes. Her mother looking worried, saying perhaps she wasn't well and should stay home from school. Her own desperate insistence that she was fine, and wanted to go—*had* to go. A blurred memory of a heart-wrenching run to school.

All the time her mind was filled with horrible pictures. Someone unpacking Mum's basket. Someone finding the black velvet bag, pulling out the Star Cloak, shaking out its glittering folds. The sunlight pouring through the long assembly hall windows. The Star Cloak crumpling, fading . . . turning into a limp, gray rag.

When she arrived at school, the playground was almost deserted, because she was so early. The parking lot was empty except for Ms. Stone's small neat, dark green car and a yellow car she'd never seen before.

She sat down on a bench that overlooked the parking lot and waited. One by one teachers arrived, parked their cars, and went up to the school. Behind her she could hear the playground filling up. There was a lot of shouting and laughing. A group started playing handball. And still there was no sign of Mrs. Tweedie.

The bell began to ring. It was time to go into class. Jessie sat where she was, gripping the rough wood of the bench.

"Better get a move on, Jessie!" Jessie jumped and spun around. Mr. Thom was walking toward her, his white teeth flashing in a cheerful smile. He had a couple of boys with him. They were watching Jessie curiously.

Mr. Thom turned to them. "The car's parked

behind the assembly hall," he said. "The lady's waiting for you. Her name's Mrs. Tweedie. Carry everything into the hall storeroom, then come straight to class."

The boys sped off. Jessie stared after them, feeling sick. She'd completely forgotten about the school's side entrance, behind the assembly hall. Those gates were usually locked. They were used only by people coming to fix things or . . . deliver things.

"Are you okay, Jess?" Mr. Thom asked. "Bell's rung, you know."

Jessie swallowed. "I—I have to see Mrs. Tweedie," she said. "We gave her something by mistake. I've got to—"

"Right now, you've got to go to class," said Mr. Thom breezily. "You can pop into the assembly hall at lunchtime. Off you go, now." And he watched her all the way to her classroom to make sure she did as she was told.

Never had Jessie gone to class so unwillingly. As she sidled through the door and went to sit in her usual place beside Sal, Ms. Stone glanced at her, but went on speaking.

". . . and as you may have heard, Petra Connelly is in the assembly hall, reading the entries for the story competition," she said. She waited for the class's excited murmuring to die down, then went on. "She'll be there all day, because there are rather a lot of entries. Unfortunately, the other local schools seem to have sent every story handed in to them, instead of choosing just a few."

"I think that's fairer," Sal whispered. "Your story should have gone in the competition, Jessie, it really—" She fell silent as Ms. Stone's icy blue gaze swept over her.

"Mrs. Connelly has a lot of reading to do, and she is *not* to be disturbed," Ms. Stone went on. "So the hall is closed to all students today. No excuses, no exceptions."

The class groaned. Jessie's heart sank to the soles of her shoes. Obviously Mr. Thom hadn't known about this. Slowly she put up her hand. "I—I have to get something we sent to the clothes stall by mistake," she said. "The clothes are in the assembly hall storeroom. Can I—?"

"I said, 'no excuses, no exceptions,' Jessica," said Ms. Stone crisply. "Your mother can ring one of the organizers tonight, and they'll put the item aside for her. Now, math books out, please . . ."

The morning dragged by. Jessie sat in a miserable daze, completely unable to concentrate. At morning break, she hung around behind some bushes near the assembly hall, waiting for a chance to slip inside. But it was impossible. The back door was locked, and Ms. Stone was keeping guard on the doors at the front. It was the same at lunchtime.

"Jessie, what's wrong?" Sal whispered when they met in the classroom after lunch. "Why are you acting so weird?"

"Sal, could you see through the assembly hall windows from where you were?" Jessie asked urgently. "Do you know if they've started going through the secondhand clothes yet?"

Sal stared at her. "That's not till after school," she said. "Ellie Lew told me. Her mother's coming. Tina Barassi's mum, too, and Mrs. Wells."

Jessie felt weak with relief. "I've got to get into

the hall, Sal," she blurted out. "I've *got* to get something from the storeroom, whatever Ms. Stone says."

Sal's eyes widened, but she didn't ask any questions. That was the great thing about Sal. All she said was, "Well, I'll help you, then. But you'll get into big trouble if you're caught."

The last class of the day was choir practice with Mrs. Klein. As soon as the bell rang signaling the end of school, Jessie and Sal grabbed their bags and ran to the assembly hall. But Ms. Stone was there before them. She stood at the front doors, jingling a bunch of keys, keeping a sharp eye on the students streaming toward the school gates.

In minutes the playground was almost empty, but Ms. Stone stayed where she was. From behind the shelter of the bushes, Jessie watched in dismay as Mrs. Lew and Mrs. Wells walked, chatting, up from the parking lot. Ms. Stone gave them the keys and they strolled on, around to the back of the hall. The sorting of the secondhand clothes was about to start.

"Jessie!" Sal hissed in her ear. "Go after Mrs. Lew. She'll leave the back door open for sure because Mrs. Barassi isn't here yet. I'll go and talk to old Stone-face, to make her look the other way. Then I'll have to go, or she'll get suspicious. Okay?"

Jessie nodded. "Thanks, Sal," she managed to say.

Sal grinned. "Good luck!" she whispered, and slipped away. Jessie watched tensely as her friend reached Ms. Stone and started talking, opening her bag and shaking her head as if she'd lost something. Sal pointed back toward the classroom, and Ms. Stone turned with her.

Now! Jessie ran to the back of the hall. Just as Sal had said, the door was ajar. Jessie peeped inside. An empty corridor stretched ahead of her. She could hear voices echoing from the front of the hall.

Her heart pounding, Jessie crept into the corridor. It was lined with doors. All were shut except the last one on the left, which was propped open by a fat bag of clothes. The storeroom!

Jessie ran along the corridor on tiptoe and darted into the storeroom, almost falling over a clutter of boxes and bags heaped just inside the doorway. She couldn't see her mother's basket, but she knew it was there. She could feel the Star Cloak. Her skin had begun to prickle, and little thrills of excitement were running through her arms and legs.

She edged around the untidy heap, straining her eyes in the dimness, and at last saw her mother's old laundry basket, right at the back. Several bags of clothes had been piled on top of it. As quietly as she could, she pushed the bags aside and plunged her hand into the basket. She found the black velvet bag, pulled it out, forced it into her jacket pocket, and zipped the pocket up.

Now all I have to do is to get out of here without being caught, Jessie thought. She crept to the storeroom doorway and peered out. The corridor was empty. Gripping her bulging pocket tightly, she began running for the back door.

She was almost there when, to her horror, she heard a bump from outside and the back door moved. Someone carrying a box was elbowing the door open. Jessie glimpsed the sleeve of a pale gray jacket, and a slim wrist with a silver watchband. Ms. Stone!

Jessie's eyes fell on a closed door just ahead of her. She leaped forward and frantically twisted the knob, praying it wasn't locked. The knob turned. Jessie plunged through the door, shut it, and leaned against it, panting.

Only then did she realize that the room wasn't empty. A pleasant-looking woman with short gray hair and glasses sat behind a cluttered desk in the center. The woman stared at Jessie, the pen in her hand poised in midair, her eyes wide with surprise.

Jessie took a breath to stammer an apology, then froze as there was a knock on the door. "It's Lyn Stone," Ms. Stone's voice said crisply.

Jessie clapped her hand over her mouth to stifle a squeak of fear. The woman behind the desk regarded her with interest. Then she put a finger to her lips and made a small sideways gesture with her other hand.

Wondering, Jessie slid aside. The door swung open, hiding her from view. She flattened herself against the wall, a cold wall heater digging into her spine.

"Here are the rest of our school's entries, Mrs. Connelly, for the display you suggested," she heard Ms. Stone say politely. "I'll just put them with the others you've already read, to keep them together."

Jessie's face began to burn. The woman behind the desk was Petra Connelly! What must she think? What was she going to do?

"Again, I must apologize for the number of entries the other schools sent," Ms. Stone said. "You must be getting very tired."

"Not at all," Petra Connelly answered cheerily. "In fact, for some reason I feel quite shivery with excitement at the moment. You're shivering, too, I see. Isn't that strange?"

They can feel the Star Cloak, Jessie thought, pressing her hands together in terror.

"It's just a little chilly in here," Ms. Stone said. "I'll turn on the heater."

"No!" Petra Connelly said quickly. "I mean . . . just have a look at this story first. It's really very good!"

Jessie heard Ms. Stone's footsteps move farther into the room. She peeped around the edge of the door. Ms. Stone was bending over the desk, reading a story written on pink paper. Petra Connelly was looking over Ms. Stone's shoulder, straight at Jessie. As Jessie stared, Petra Connelly winked and jerked her head slightly.

The message was clear. Jessie edged out from behind the door and crept to the doorway. She mouthed "thank you," then slipped out of the room. In seconds she had reached the back door and let herself out into the deserted playground. Expecting every moment to hear Ms. Stone calling her name, she fled to the bushes, picked up her bag, and pounded toward the school gate.

Jogging home, she thought her terrible day was nearly over, but she was wrong. As she rounded the corner into her own street, she saw the car pulling out of Blue Moon, her mother at the wheel. The car came to an abrupt stop beside her.

"Jessie, where have you been?" Rosemary exclaimed, throwing open the passenger door. "I was coming to find you. Get in! I managed to get an appointment at the hairdresser for you, but it's in forty minutes, and I have to do all the shopping first."

Jessie found her voice. "Mum, no!" she panted. "I have to—I don't need a haircut."

"Of course you do," said Rosemary. "It's all hanging in your eyes. That's probably what's giving you these headaches. Hurry up, now!"

I should just run, Jessie thought frantically. I should just run to the secret garden, disappear into the Realm, and explain later. That's what a kid in a movie would do.

But this wasn't a movie. This was real life, and Rosemary was waiting, tapping the wheel impatiently. Almost crying with frustration, Jessie got into the car.

# wish Night

When at last Jessie and her mother got back to Blue Moon, the sun was going down. It was nearly time for Wish Night to begin.

Queen Helena must know the Cloak's missing by now, Jessie thought as she heaved bags of groceries out of the car and ran to the house. She'll be frantic! On Stardust Mountain, the workers will be getting ready to gather the stardust. And Flash and her warriors will be swarming out of the Cavern, hunting for poor Giff. Oh, I have to *hurry*!

Granny turned from the kitchen window to greet them as they came in. She looked rather pale, but the moment she laid eyes on Jessie's backpack, her green eyes flashed, and Jessie knew that she felt the Star Cloak's magic. Jessie's heart leaped. Granny would help her. Granny would—

"Two little friends of yours came while you were out, Jessie," Granny said. "They were very sorry to have missed you."

Jessie's eyes widened. Granny was looking at her intently. Obviously the "two little friends" were Maybelle and Patrice. In desperation they'd come to Granny for help. How astonished they must have been to hear that Jessie had been home all day!

Jessie began to edge toward the back door. "They might still be hanging around," she said. "I'll just go and—"

"No!" Rosemary said firmly. "I want you to go and lie down, Jessie. You've been miserable all afternoon. You might be getting the flu or something. I feel a bit shivery myself, actually."

Jessie glanced at her grandmother for help, but to her surprise and dismay, Granny shook her head. "It's too late to go into the garden now, Jessie," she said. "I saw the first star a minute ago. Very soon, the sky will be full of them. It's just too late."

A painful lump rose in Jessie's throat. *Too late.* Granny was telling her that she'd never get from the secret Door to the palace in time to save Wish Night, or Giff.

"My advice is to do what your mum says and go to your room for a while," Granny said, slowly and clearly. "You'll be able to see the first star from your window, and you can make a wish. That will make you feel better, won't it?"

Jessie's heart leaped as she understood what Granny was telling her. Of course! Why hadn't she thought of it herself? She nodded quickly and darted out of the kitchen.

In moments she was closing the door of her room behind her. The curtains were open to the darkening sky. She took the velvet bag from her backpack and gently pulled out the Star Cloak. It looked perfect. She couldn't even see where the ugly tear had been.

The Cloak whispered around her, cool and tingling, as she put it on. The strings tied easily, as if they were tying themselves. She ran to the window and looked out at the first star. "I wish I was in the palace with Queen Helena," she whispered, and cool, blue shadows closed in around her.

The next moment, three joyful voices were shrilling in her ears, and eager hands were helping her to her feet. She stood, swaying, as the Star Cloak was taken from her shoulders.

When at last her eyes came back into focus, she saw that she was in the great entrance hall of the palace. Patrice was clinging to her arm. Maybelle was on her other side, pawing the ground with excitement. And Queen Helena was standing before her, wearing a flowing dress of silver, a sparkling silver crown, and the Star Cloak, blue as the blue moon and shimmering with magic.

Except for the four of them, the entrance hall was empty. The great, golden front doors were closed.

"Am I in time?" Jessie managed to ask.

Queen Helena hugged her. It was like being hugged by moonlight that smelled of flowers. "Just in time," Helena whispered. "I knew you'd do it somehow, Jessie. I never lost hope."

"Neither did I, dearie," said Patrice loyally.

"I did," snorted Maybelle, shaking her mane. "I've aged ten years in the last ten minutes. And where, may I ask, is that fool of an elf who caused all this?"

Jessie felt a stab of panic as she suddenly remembered. "Giff's lost on Stardust Mountain," she said urgently. "The star fairy warriors are really angry with him. They're hunting him! We've got to help him. He's—"

"Later, we will talk," Queen Helena said quickly. "There is no time now." She turned and held up her hand.

The golden doors swung open, revealing the broad palace steps and the huge crowd gathered on the ground below. Queen Helena walked out of the palace to stand smiling on the topmost step with the Star Cloak swirling around her. The crowd gave a mighty roar. Fairies, elves, gnomes, pixies, sprites, dwarfs, miniature horses, the tall beautiful people called the Folk, and hundreds of other magical beings Jessie had never seen before, were cheering as one.

But this was not what made Jessie gasp in awe. It was the sky—the sky ablaze with stars that were so huge, so bright, that the whole, vast canopy looked like a twinkling mass of silver and gold.

"Quickly!" snapped Maybelle. "Outside, or we'll miss out on the wishes!"

The wishes, Jessie thought. Of course! I can wish, too. I can have anything I want—anything that's possible, Giff said. But here in the Realm, almost anything's possible. Almost anything . . .

No one noticed Jessie, Patrice, and Maybelle slip silently through the doorway, and hurry down one side of the stairs. The crowd had eyes only for their Queen.

The Star Cloak swirled and glittered. Queen Helena raised her arms to the sky. Everyone looked up. The stars above them seemed to lean closer. Then, with a strange, beautiful sound, like sighing music, stars began to fall, swooping downward like enormous birds, their trailing tails of silver light making swirling patterns in the sky. Jessie watched, transfixed. Her ears were filled with the music of the falling stars. She was shivering all over.

"Now," she heard Patrice whisper. "Remember, Jessie. Wish for the thing you want most. The dearest wish of your heart."

The sky music rose. One of the stars burst in a shower of sparks. Then another did the same, and another. The sky was filled with blazing light. The crowd cried out as glittering stardust began to fall like rain.

Then there was silence, except for the singing of the stars, and Jessie knew that all around her people were wishing.

*. . . the thing you want most. The dearest wish of your heart.*

There were so many things she could wish for. But as the stardust settled on her face and hands, and spangled her hair, she knew that there was only one thing that really mattered. She shut her eyes and wished, with all her heart, for Giff to come home.

She repeated her wish many times. Then she realized that the star music had died away. Slowly she opened her eyes again. The falling stars had gone. The air around her was filled with glittering specks of light. Everywhere fairy folk were dancing and clapping, while above them arched the canopy of the sky, black velvet sprinkled with tiny diamonds.

Jessie looked around quickly. Maybelle's mane and tail were frosted with starlight. Patrice's face was glowing. But there was no sign of Giff. The lump rose in Jessie's throat again. She had so hoped. . . .

"What's the matter, dearie?" Patrice asked anxiously. "Surely you didn't forget to wish?"

"No. But . . . but my wish hasn't come true," Jessie whispered, fighting back her tears.

Maybelle whisked her tail, showering Patrice with more stardust. "You can't expect miracles, you know," she said. "I mean, things don't just appear out of thin air just because you wish for them. That's not how it works. You often have to wait—for quite a long time, sometimes. And you never know exactly how it's going to happen. Giff wished for the Star Cloak to be mended, didn't he? In the end it was—but not in the way he meant."

"Once, Giff wished for his hair to turn blue." Patrice giggled. "He was really disappointed when it didn't. Then, a couple of months later, he fell into a tub of blue rainbow crystals in the storehouse."

"His hair turned blue then, all right!" Maybelle snorted. "So did the rest of him. He was completely blue for days. What a sight he was!"

She and Patrice laughed, and even Jessie smiled. But the laughter died away quickly. Maybelle cleared her throat uncomfortably, and Patrice's round face grew troubled. Jessie knew they were both wondering if they would ever see their friend again.

She couldn't bear it. Quickly she turned away and looked up at the sky. It was hard to believe that only minutes ago it had been exploding with silver light. It looked completely normal now. At least . . .

Jessie frowned, and shook her head. For a moment it had looked as if some of the new stars were moving. My eyes are playing tricks on me, she thought. But when she looked again, she saw exactly what she had seen before. Hundreds of stars, packed tightly together, were speeding toward the palace.

# surprises

"Patrice, Maybelle, look!" Jessie gasped. "More stars are falling."

"Oh no, Jessie, that's all over," murmured Patrice. "There are only new stars in the sky now, and they— Oh!"

"What in the Realm . . . ?" said Maybelle, at the same moment.

They had both looked up at last. They had seen the glittering mass shooting toward them. Others in the crowd had seen it, too. Everywhere there were shouts of surprise and alarm.

"What's happening?" squeaked Patrice.

"I don't know," muttered Maybelle, pawing the ground nervously. "I've never heard of new stars acting like this. They're coming at us very fast, too. I think we should—"

But Patrice and Jessie never found out what Maybelle thought they should do. Because at that very moment the mass of light streaked down from the sky like a huge, humming arrow, and something crashed to the ground between them, knocking them all sprawling.

Everyone was screaming. Her head spinning, her ears ringing, Jessie crawled to her knees, trying to understand what had happened. She saw the arrow of light speeding away across the sky. She saw the milling crowd of fairy folk parting to make way as Queen Helena came running. She saw Patrice and Maybelle lying gasping on the ground, all the breath knocked out of them. And right beside her, whimpering, scratched, bedraggled, and covered in mud, was . . .

"Giff!" Jessie squealed. She threw her arms around the elf, and hugged him tight. "Oh, Giff, you're home! My wish came true!"

"*Your* wish?" cried Patrice. "Goodness, Jessie, that was *my* wish, too."

"And mine," Maybelle admitted gruffly. "I was going to wish for a nice, juicy patch of four-leafed clover, but I missed Giff, for some reason, so I wished for him instead. I must have been out of my mind."

Patrice laughed. "No wonder you arrived in such a rush, Giff," she said. "Three wishes, all for you!"

"Four, actually," said a gentle voice. "I wished for Giff to come home, too." Everyone looked up and saw Queen Helena smiling down at them. Patrice, Maybelle, and Jessie scrambled to their feet. Giff moaned, and covered his muddy face with his hands.

"Oh dear, oh dear," he wailed. "You all wasted your wishes on me! And I'm not worth it! I'm so sorry I tore the Star Cloak, Queen Helena! I'm so sorry I ran away! I'm so sorry I put Jessie in danger! I was just so scared when Loris and the guards came after me—"

"Giff!" Queen Helena shook her head and bent

105

to pull the little elf to his feet. "Last night, I didn't even know the Star Cloak was missing! The guards were only trying to find you because the griffins were causing trouble, and you had the last box of griffin treats."

Giff's jaw dropped. He felt inside his jacket and pulled out a very crumpled yellow box decorated with a picture of a smiling griffin. "Oh," he said weakly. "I forgot."

"I don't believe it!" groaned Maybelle.

"Oh, leave him alone," said Patrice. "He's been punished enough."

"I agree," Queen Helena said quietly. "But from now on, Giff, come and *tell* me if something bad happens, even if it's your fault. If you'd done that last night, I could have taken the Cloak to Stardust Mountain myself, and you and Jessie and all of us would have been saved a lot of worry and trouble."

"Yes, Giff. It's very lucky that when the star fairy warriors found you, they agreed to bring you home," Patrice put in. "They could have hurt you very badly."

"One of them nearly did," snuffled Giff. "Her name was Flash, and she was really fierce. But another one called Gleam stopped her. Gleam said that Jessie had forgiven Flash for attacking her, so Flash should forgive *me* for damaging the Star Cloak. Gleam said that would make Jessie glad, and pay back what Flash owed her."

He wiped his eyes with the back of his hand and sniffed again. "Gleam talked and talked and finally the others agreed—even Flash. And they were just about to go away and leave me in the awful, muddy hole they found me in, when the stars started falling. Then all of them suddenly got really happy and excited, and somehow they got the idea to carry me home."

"Thanks to our wishes," Maybelle said sourly.

"Only the coming-home part," Patrice said, putting her arm around Giff. "The coming-home-*safe* part was all thanks to Jessie."

"You look *so* much better this morning, Jessie," Rosemary said, at breakfast. "You must have had a good night."

"Oh, I *did*." Jessie sighed. It was true, though she was sure that feasting and celebrating till midnight in the Realm wasn't the sort of "good night" her mother meant.

She went to the Spring Fair feeling as if a huge weight had rolled off her shoulders. When the time came, she stood on the assembly hall stage with the rest of the choir, and sang with real joy. But when Petra Connelly came on stage with Ms. Stone to announce the winners of the story competition, Jessie felt herself beginning to blush, and edged a little behind Sal. The thought of the narrow escape she'd had in the hall yesterday still made her stomach turn over.

Ms. Stone made a speech welcoming Petra Connelly. Then Petra Connelly spoke about the high standard of the stories and said how much she'd enjoyed the judging. Then she said it was time to announce the winner. And she called Jessie's name.

For a moment, Jessie didn't move. She was sure that she'd imagined it.

"Jessie!" hissed Sal, nudging her violently. "Jessie, it's you! Go on!"

Astounded, Jessie stumbled from her place and walked to the front of the stage. Everyone was clapping, especially the choir. When Petra Connelly saw Jessie, her eyes widened in surprise, then she beamed.

"Well, well," she murmured, shaking Jessie's hand and giving her the big parcel of books that was the competition's first prize. "So we meet again."

"I . . . I think there's been a mistake," Jessie stammered, knowing her face must be bright red. "My story wasn't one of the finalists. It was about — about a unicorn." She glanced over her shoulder. Ms. Stone's face was rigid.

"That's the one!" exclaimed Petra Connelly, in a louder voice, so that Ms. Stone, and the whole audience, could hear her. "The unicorn story. Wonderful! It was in the box of entries Ms. Stone brought in after school."

"Yes," said Ms. Stone, through tight lips.

"You see," said Petra Connelly, her smile broadening, "I felt so full of energy after . . . after your visit, Ms. Stone, that I decided to look at all the entries in that box, as well as the others I had. Why not? I thought. You never know. And, after all, I am the judge."

She smiled at Ms. Stone, completely ignoring her obvious annoyance. "And as soon as I read the unicorn story, I knew I had my winner," she went on. "It was about fantastic things, of course, but while I was reading it, I really believed it. You believed it, too, while you were writing it, didn't you, Jessica?"

"Oh, yes," Jessie said. "Completely!"

"And that's the sign of a real writer," said Petra Connelly. "Keep it up!"

Then everyone clapped again, and Ms. Stone had no choice but to make her speech of thanks and watch Petra Connelly being presented with a bunch of flowers, just as if she wasn't furious but felt absolutely fine.

"Old Stone-face must be so angry." Sal giggled as she and Jessie left the hall after it was all over. "I hope she doesn't pick on you even more now."

Jessie shook her head. She knew that in a way Ms. Stone was like the star fairy warriors. She was cold, but she was fair. She wouldn't allow herself the weakness of showing her feelings. And her logical mind would tell her that the whole thing had been Petra Connelly's fault, not Jessie's.

But Jessie was sure that if it hadn't been for the Star Cloak, and that restless, excited feeling it gave everyone around it, Petra Connelly would never have opened the box Ms. Stone brought to her room. Then she would never have read the unicorn story.

So really I won the competition because the Star Cloak was lost, Jessie thought. It's so strange. But Ms. Stone doesn't know about the Star Cloak. And even if I told her about it, she wouldn't believe me. Poor Ms. Stone.

"So," Sal was saying with satisfaction. "Everything worked out really well in the end, didn't it?"

"Yes," Jessie said. "It did."

She thought of the star fairies, sleeping contentedly after their long night's work. She thought of Giff, safe at home again. She thought of the Star Cloak, back in the Realm treasure house for another year. She thought of the tiny gold star that Queen Helena had fastened to her charm bracelet before wishing her home. She thought of what her mother would say, when she heard about the prize.

And smiling, she walked with Sal out into the sun.

Turn the page for a peek at
Jessie's next adventure in the

# Fairy Realm:

## BOOK 8

# The water sprites

J essie fastened her charm bracelet around her wrist and checked her reflection in the mirror. Her green eyes were sparkling. Her golden red hair shone against the rich blue of her new dress. She looked happy and excited, and no wonder! It was a sunny Saturday afternoon, and she was going to a party. Not an ordinary party, either, but a party in the magical world of the Realm.

The charm bracelet jingled softly as Jessie picked up the gold-speckled leaf lying beside her hairbrush. When she'd found the leaf on her desk a couple of days before, she'd thought at first that it was quite ordinary. She thought the breeze had blown it through her open window.

She'd never seen a leaf just like it before, but that wasn't surprising. The garden of Blue Moon, her grandmother's old house in the mountains, was filled with unusual trees and bushes. Though she and her mother had been living with Granny for more than a year, Jessie was still discovering plants that were new to her.

But when she picked up the speckled leaf, she suddenly saw that there was something strange about it. The yellow speckles were in straight lines, set tidily one above the other. Jessie peered at them closely. And then she realized that the speckles were words! The leaf was covered in tiny yellow writing.

Jessie smiled as she remembered how astonished and delighted she'd been as she read the leaf's message for the first time.

*Princess Jessie! The village of Lirralee invites you to baby Jewel's Welcome Party on Saturday afternoon. The party begins at three o'clock, and ends when the birds go to bed. There will be music, dancing, games, and lots of food. Please come!*

On the other side of the leaf there was another message, in different handwriting.

*Hope you can come, Jessie. Giff and Maybelle are invited, too. Be at my place at 2:30 and we can all go together. Lirralee is my old home village. Everyone is longing to meet you. Love, Patrice.*

Jessie had been very relieved to read that note. She had no idea where Lirralee was, but with her friends Patrice, the palace housekeeper, Giff the elf, and Maybelle the miniature horse to guide her, she wouldn't get lost.

She glanced at the clock on her bedside table and was startled to see that it was after two o'clock. Time had flown. If she didn't hurry, she'd be late. She grabbed the gift she'd wrapped in silver paper, and hurried out of her room to find her grandmother.

Voices were floating from the kitchen. Jessie sighed as she recognized the chirping tones of Mrs. Tweedie, the next-door neighbor.

What a nuisance! Mrs. Tweedie was a very curious woman. If she saw Jessie heading for the bottom of the Blue Moon garden dressed in party clothes, she'd ask all sorts of questions.

Jessie hesitated, wondering if she should just slip out the front door without saying goodbye. Her mother was out for the day, and Granny would understand.

"I'm so upset!" Mrs. Tweedie wailed. "I was terribly fond of that ring. It was my mother's."

"I'm sure you'll find it, Louise," Granny said

5

soothingly. "It's probably just fallen—"

"No!" Mrs. Tweedie insisted. "It was on my bedside table, in a little crystal dish. I remember *perfectly*. I put it there before I did the washing. I *always* put it there. That Wiseman person who came to clean the windows took it. I *know* he did."

Jessie's eyes widened, and she felt heat rush into her face. Mr. Wiseman was the father of her friend Sal. He was a kind, cheerful man, always full of jokes and fun, just like Sal. What was Mrs. Tweedie saying about him?

She rushed into the kitchen. Granny and Mrs. Tweedie turned to look at her.

"Is that a new outfit, dear?" asked Mrs. Tweedie, her sharp little nose twitching as she looked Jessie up and down. "I don't think I've seen it before. It's very pretty. Are you going to a party?"

"Yes," Jessie said breathlessly. "But, Mrs. Tweedie, I couldn't help hearing what you were saying about Mr. Wiseman just now, and—"

Mrs. Tweedie's face grew solemn. "It's not very nice, I know," she said. "I hate to accuse anyone, but facts are facts. I can't go to the police—I mean,

6

the man will just deny he took my ring, won't he? But I know he did it, and it's only right to warn people about him."

"Louise, believe me, Alf Wiseman is no thief!" Granny said, very firmly. "He's been in and out of Blue Moon for years—ever since he started his window-cleaning business. He's as honest as the day is long."

"Of course he is!" Jessie exclaimed. "He's my friend's dad. I know him really well."

Mrs. Tweedie looked at her sorrowfully. "I *am* sorry, dear," she said. "But, sadly, people aren't always what they seem."

"Jessie, you'd better go, or you'll be late," Granny said, as Jessie opened her mouth to argue. "You'll have to run as it is."